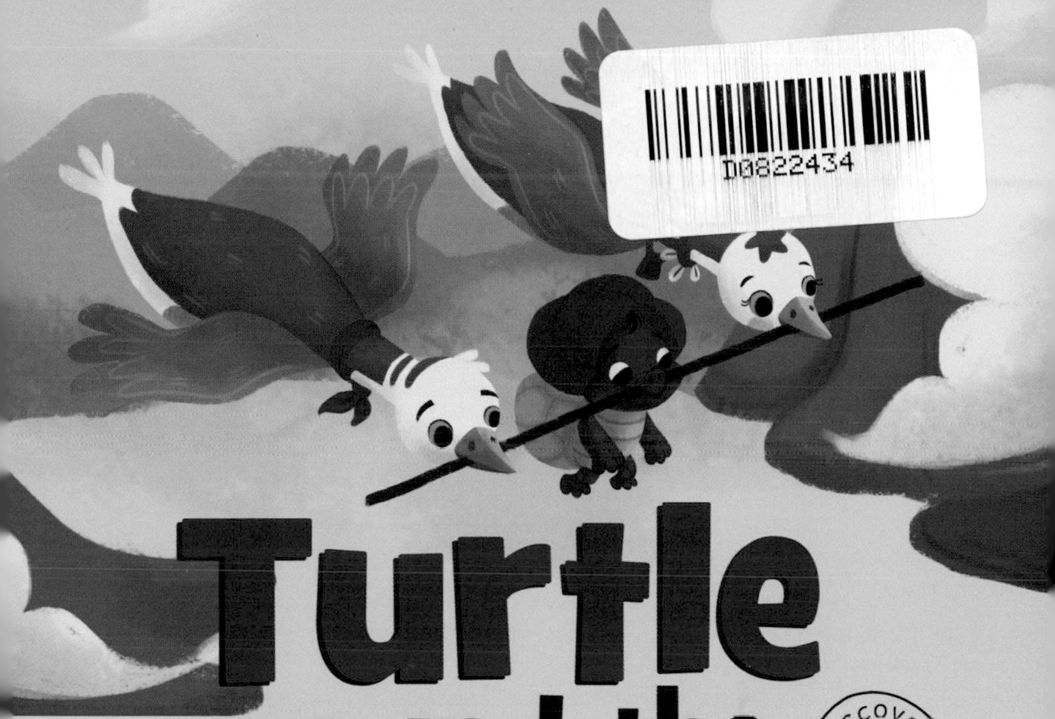

Turtle and the Geese

An Indian Graphic Folktale

BY CHITRA SOUNDAR

ILLUSTRATED BY DARSHIKA VARMA

PICTURE WINDOW BOOKS
a capstone imprint

Published by Picture Window Books,
an imprint of Capstone
1710 Roe Crest Drive
North Mankato, Minnesota 56003
capstonepub.com

Library of Congress Cataloging-in-Publication Data is
available on the Library of Congress website.
ISBN: 9781666340884 (hardcover)
ISBN: 9781666340891 (paperback)
ISBN: 9781666340907 (ebook PDF)

Summary: In this Indian folktale, a young turtle shares
a shallow lake with unlikely friends—two geese. But
when the lake starts drying up, the stubborn turtle must
follow his winged friends' advice, or he'll be left out
to dry. With fun-filled text and simple, easy-to-follow
panels, Discover Graphics: Global Folktales are perfect
for graphic novel fans, new and old.

Designed by Kay Fraser

Printed and bound in the USA. 4882

CAST OF CHARACTERS

Spot is a spotted pond turtle. He lives in a small, shrinking lake near a faraway kingdom.

Stripe is a gander with gray stripes on his head. He often travels to a beautiful lake outside the kingdom walls. He is friends with Spot the Turtle.

Star is a goose with a gray star on her head. She always travels with Stripe. Star is also friends with Spot the Turtle.

HOW TO READ A GRAPHIC NOVEL

Graphic novels are easy to read. Boxes called panels show you how to follow the story. Look at the panels from left to right and top to bottom.

Read the word boxes and word balloons from left to right as well. Don't forget the sound and action words in the pictures.

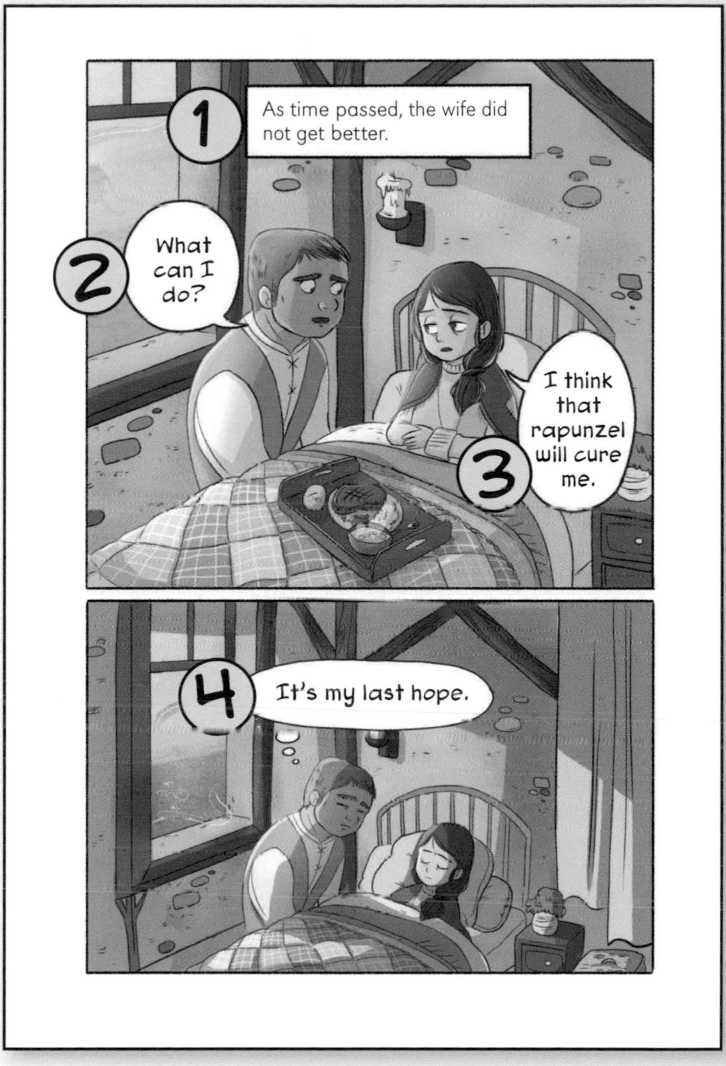
1
As time passed, the wife did not get better.
2
What can I do?
3
I think that rapunzel will cure me.
4
It's my last hope.

The pictures and the words work together to tell the whole story.

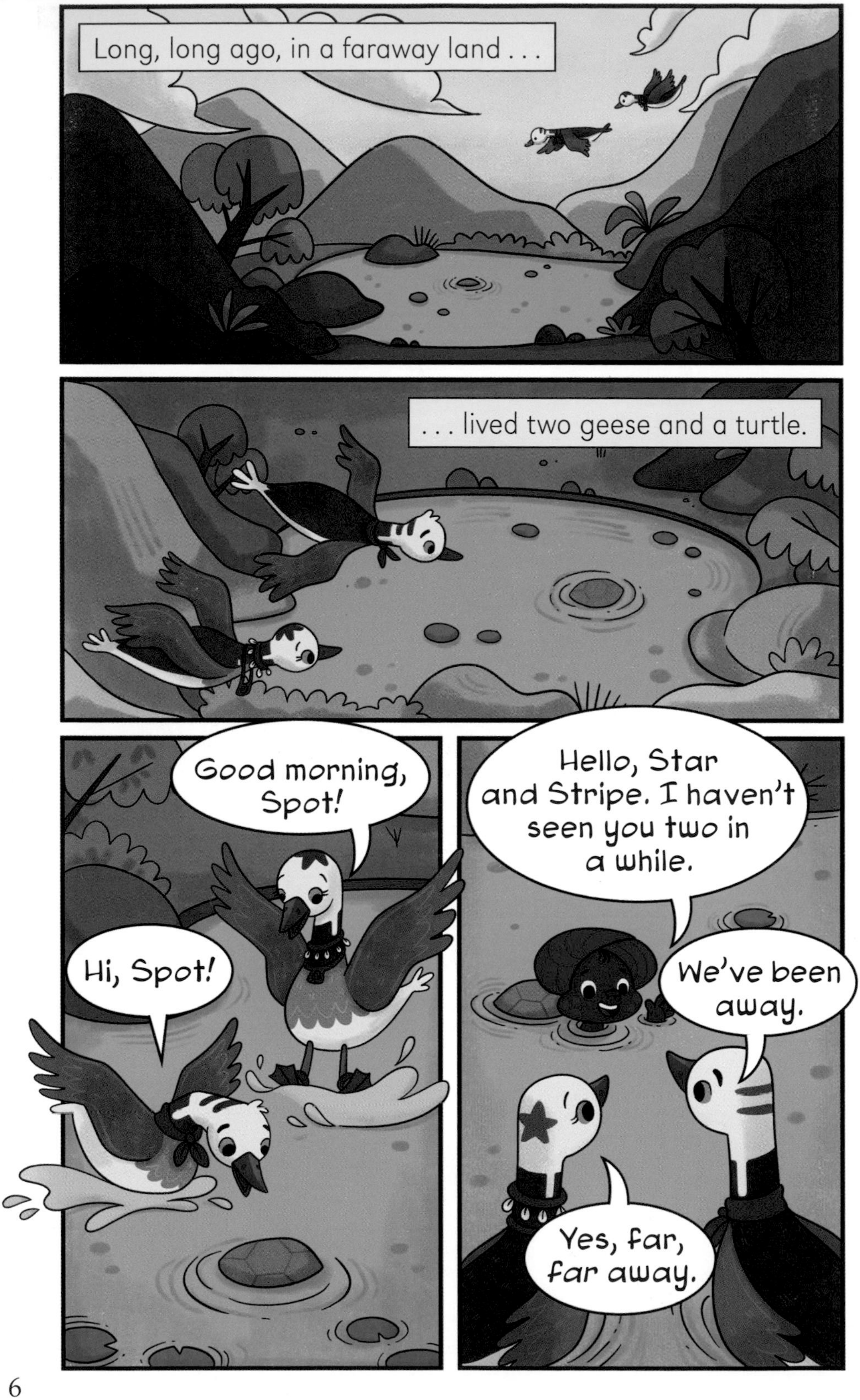

Long, long ago, in a faraway land . . .
. . . lived two geese and a turtle.
Good morning, Spot!
Hi, Spot!
Hello, Star and Stripe. I haven't seen you two in a while.
We've been away.
Yes, far, far away.

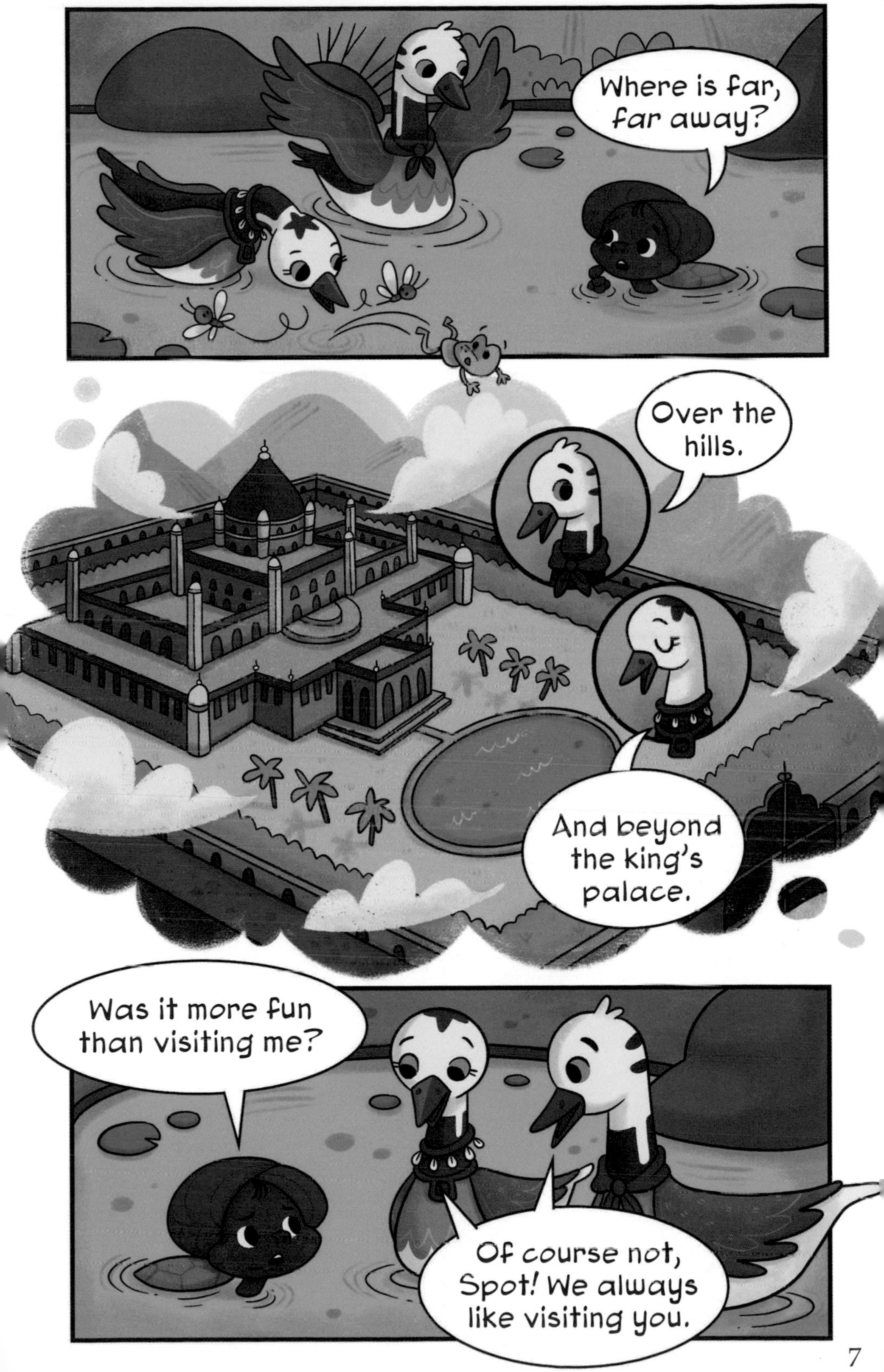
Where is far, far away?
Over the hills.
And beyond the king's palace.
Was it more fun than visiting me?
Of course not, Spot! We always like visiting you.

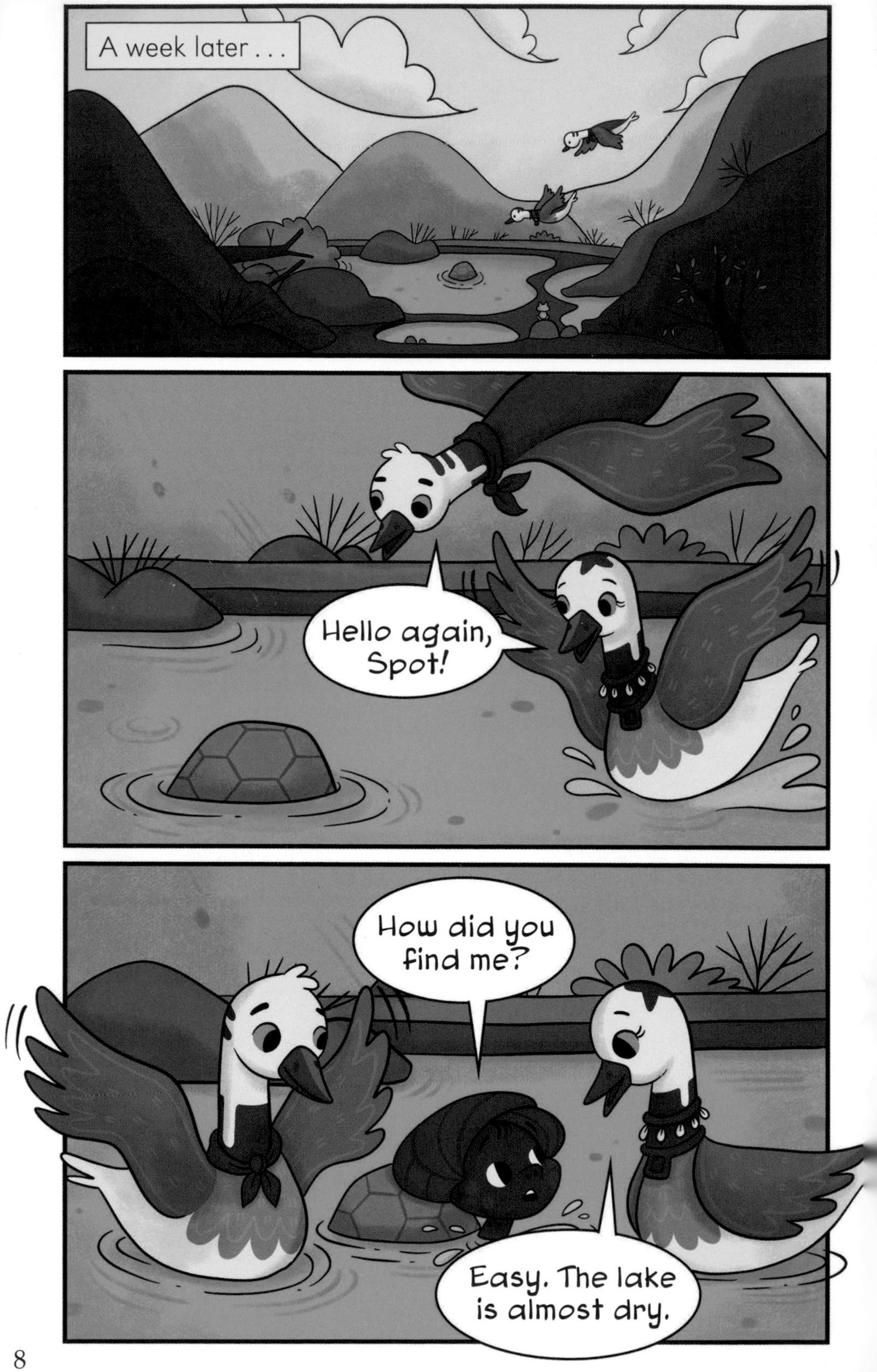
A week later . . .
Hello again, Spot!
How did you find me?
Easy. The lake is almost dry.

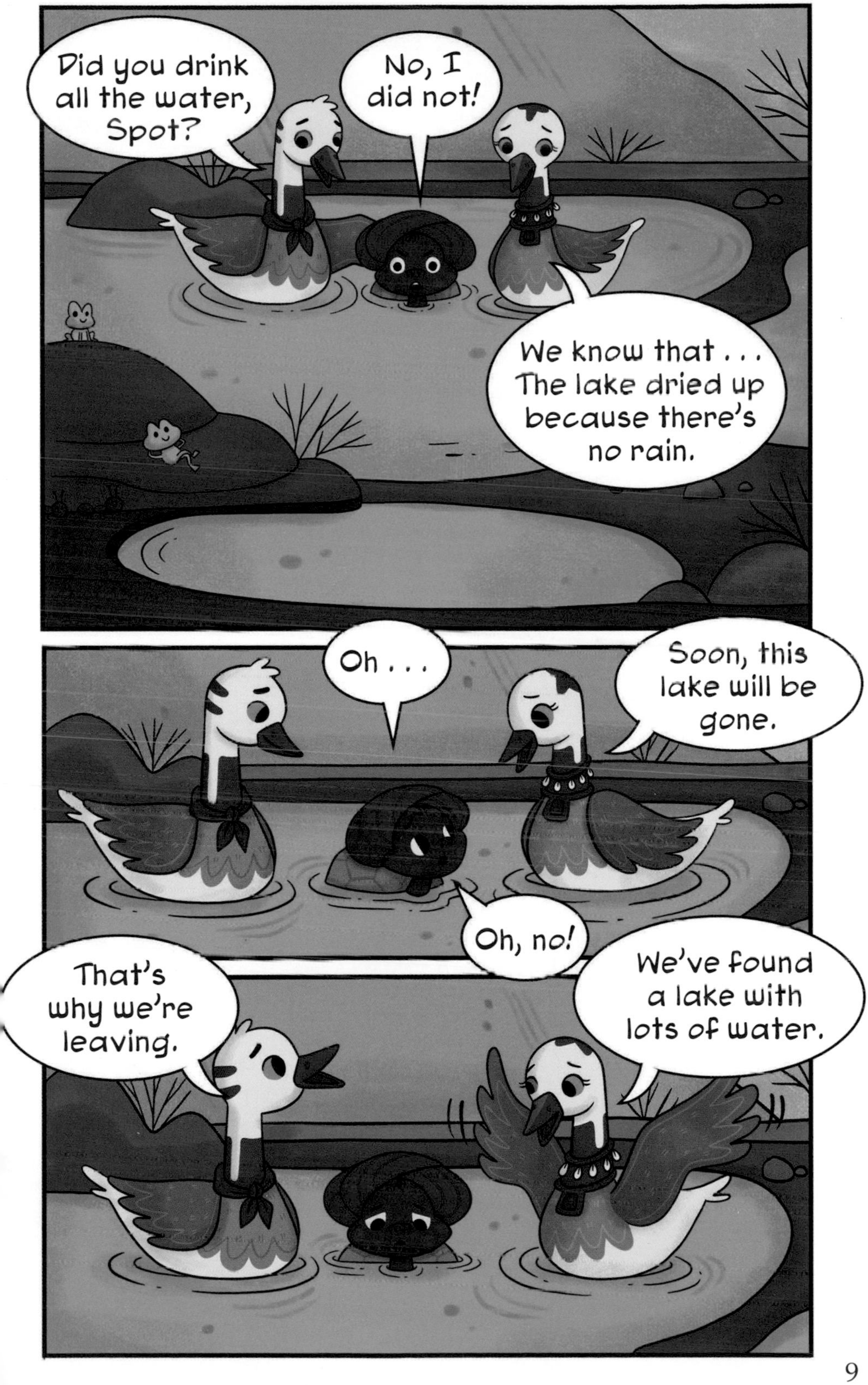
Did you drink all the water, Spot?
No, I did not!
We know that . . . The lake dried up because there's no rain.
Oh . . .
Soon, this lake will be gone.
Oh, no!
That's why we're leaving.
We've found a lake with lots of water.

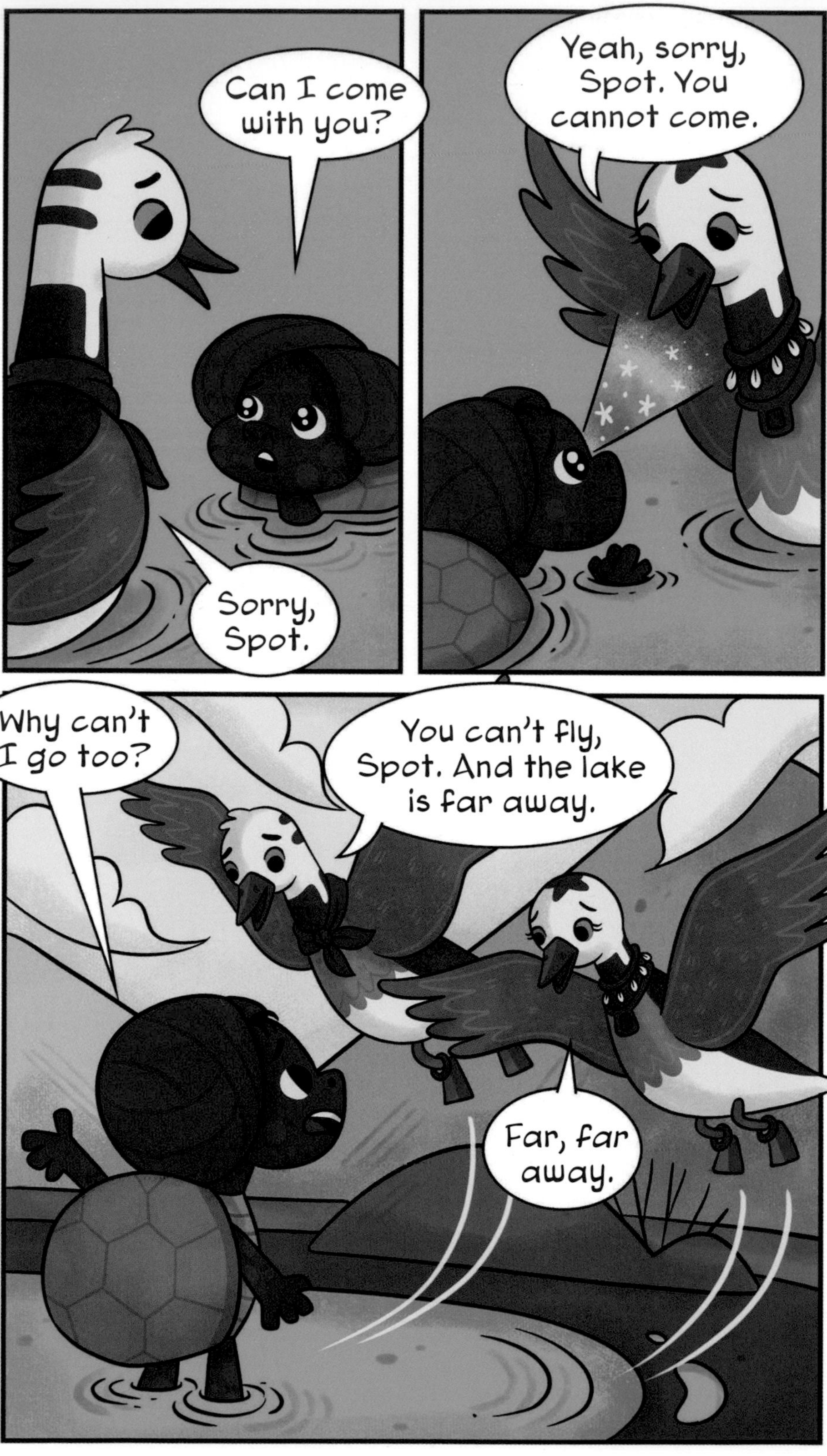
Can I come with you?
Sorry, Spot.
Yeah, sorry, Spot. You cannot come.
Why can't I go too?
You can't fly, Spot. And the lake is far away.
Far, far away.

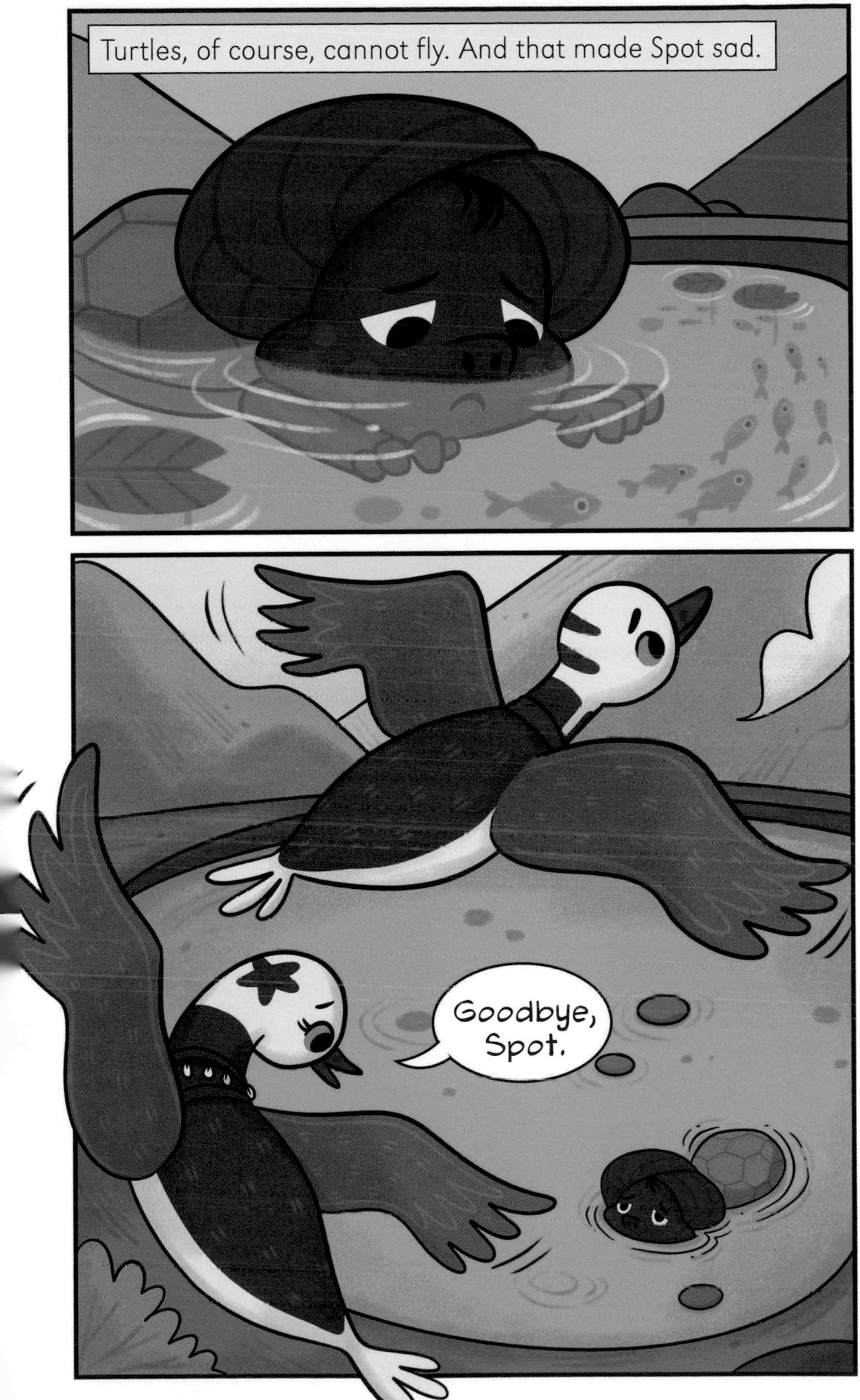
Turtles, of course, cannot fly. And that made Spot sad.
Goodbye, Spot.

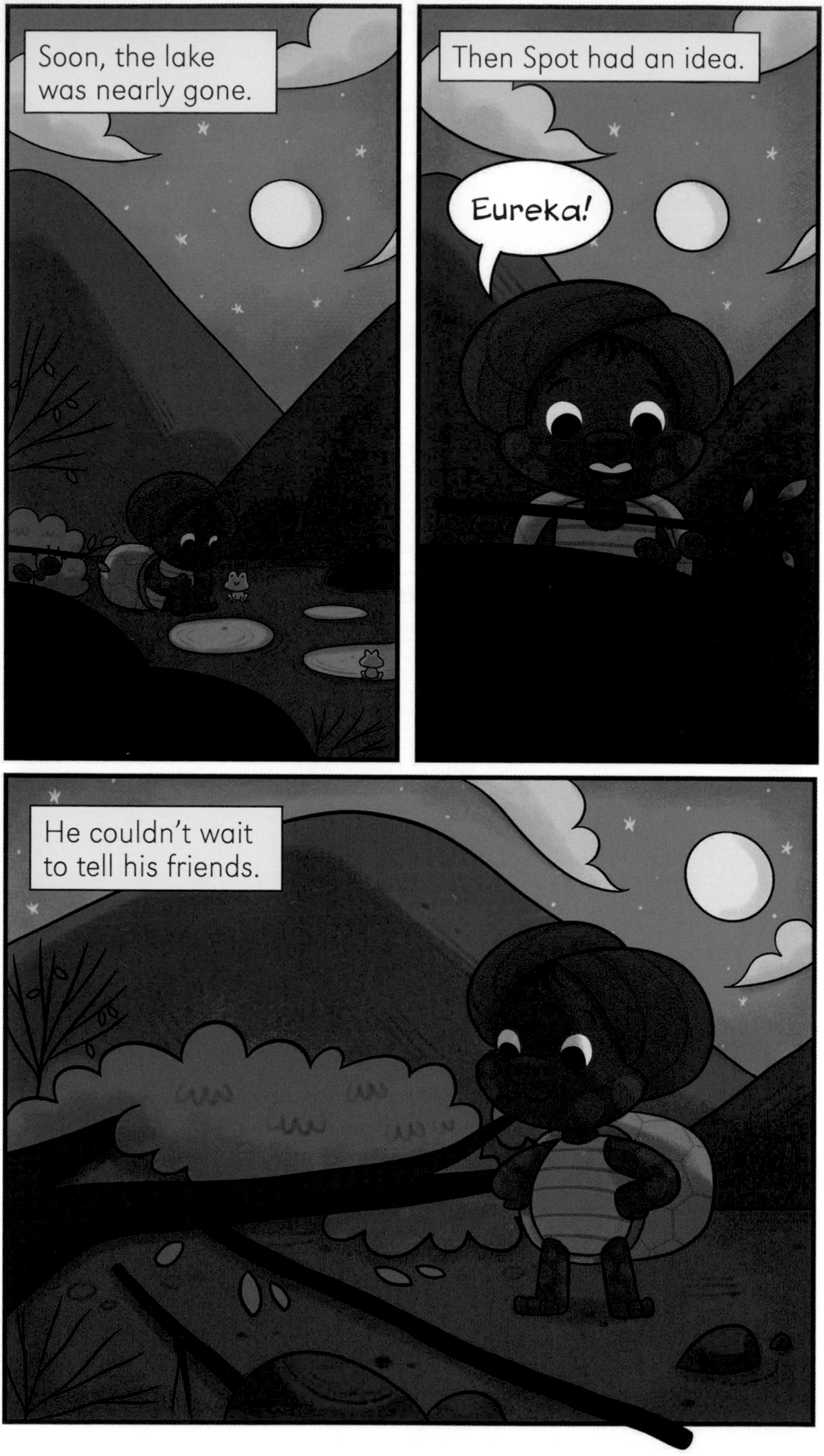
Soon, the lake was nearly gone.
Then Spot had an idea.
Eureka!
He couldn't wait to tell his friends.

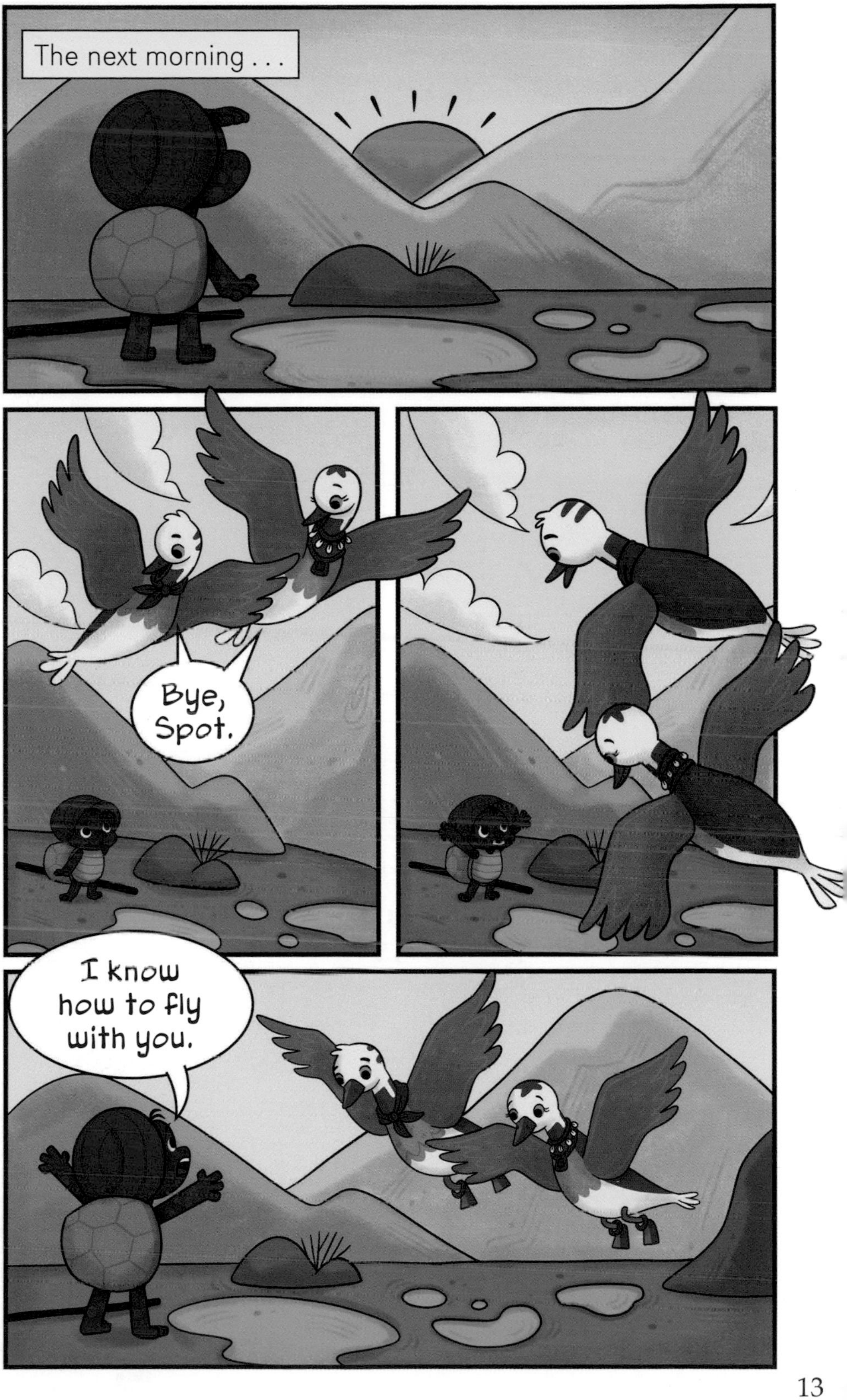
The next morning . . .
Bye, Spot.
I know how to fly with you.

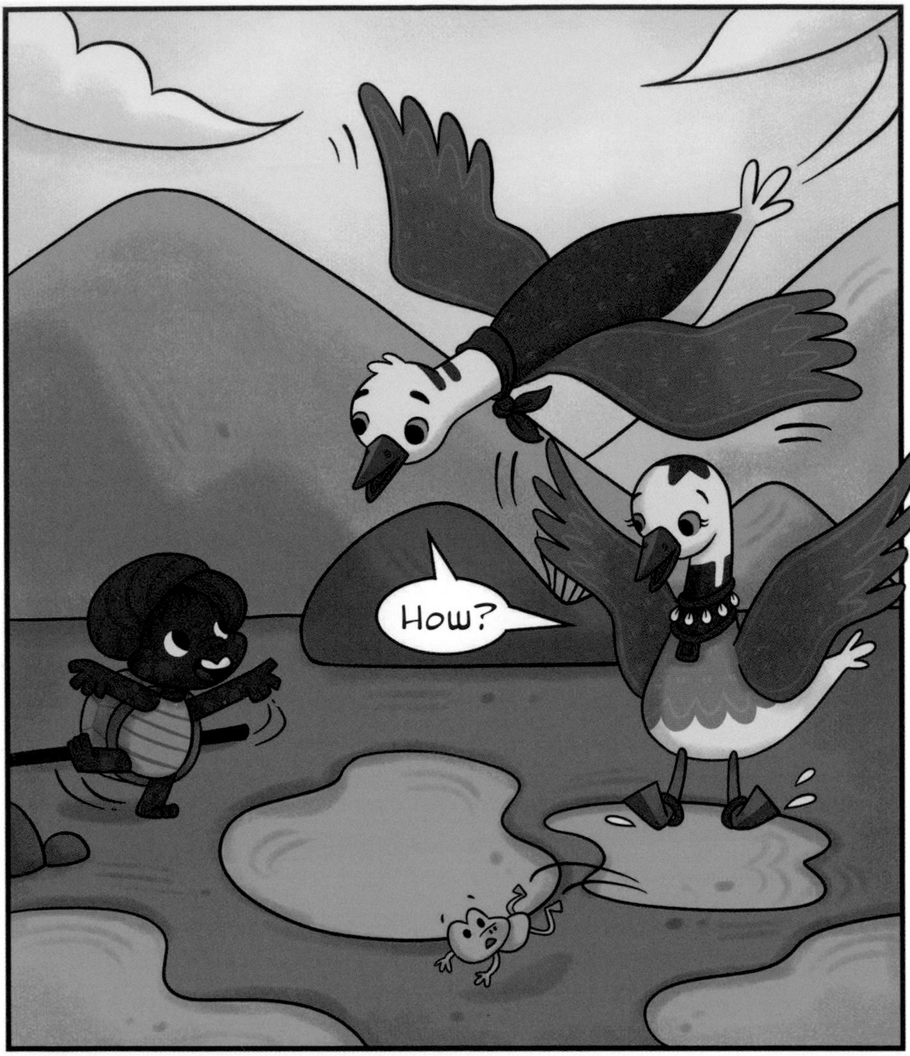
How?

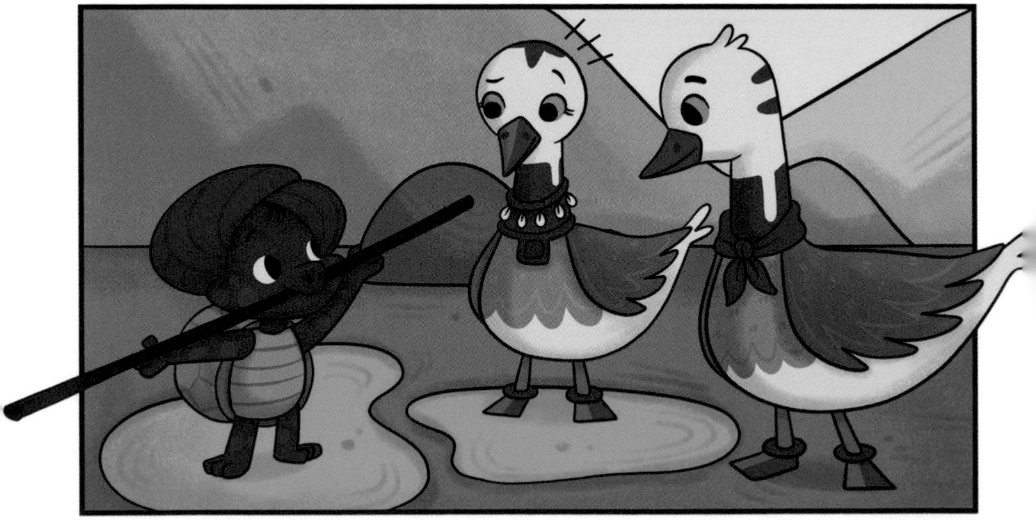

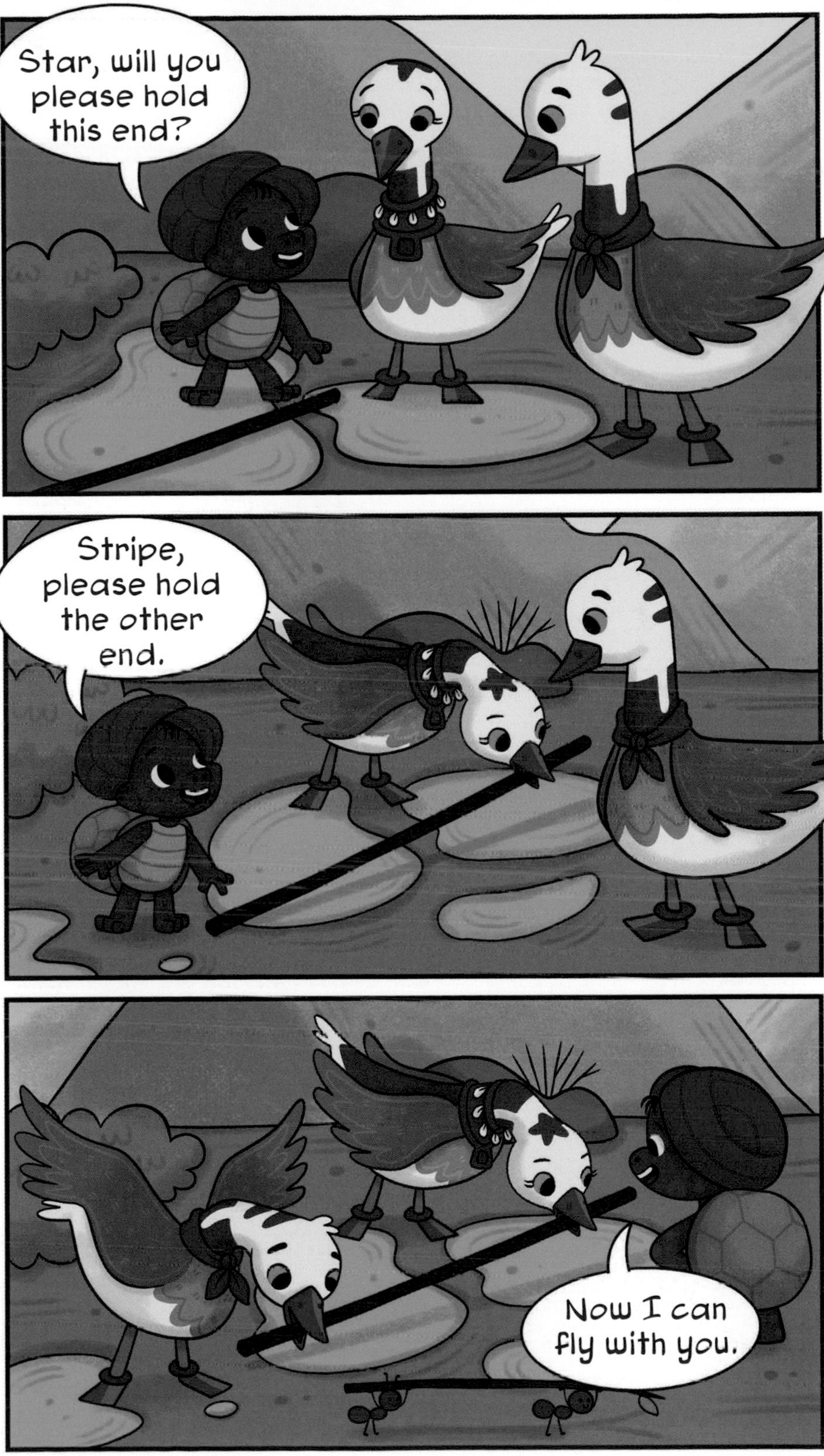
Star, will you please hold this end?
Stripe, please hold the other end.
Now I can fly with you.

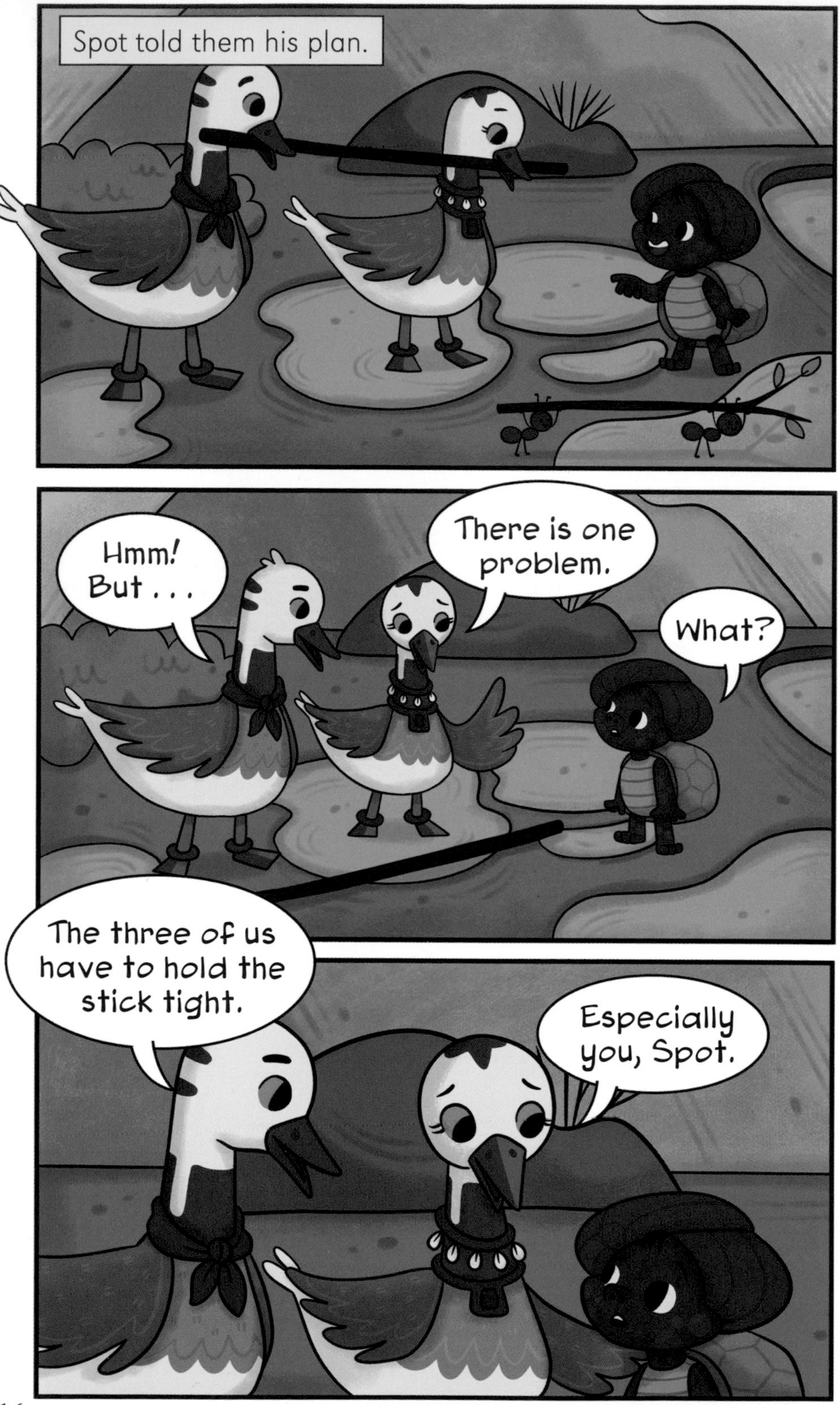
Spot told them his plan.
Hmm! But . . .
There is one problem.
What?
The three of us have to hold the stick tight.
Especially you, Spot.

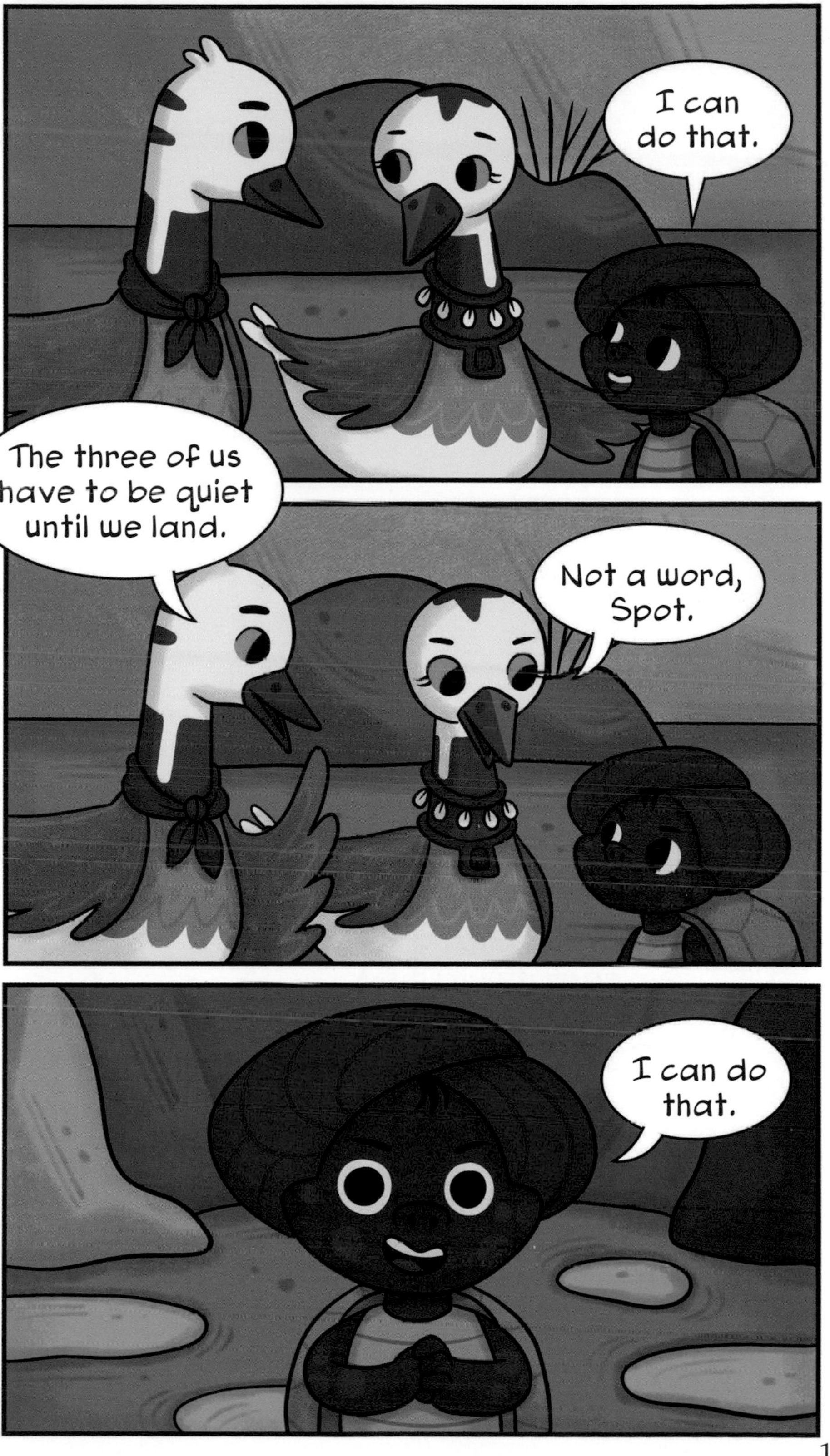
I can do that.
The three of us have to be quiet until we land.
Not a word, Spot.
I can do that.

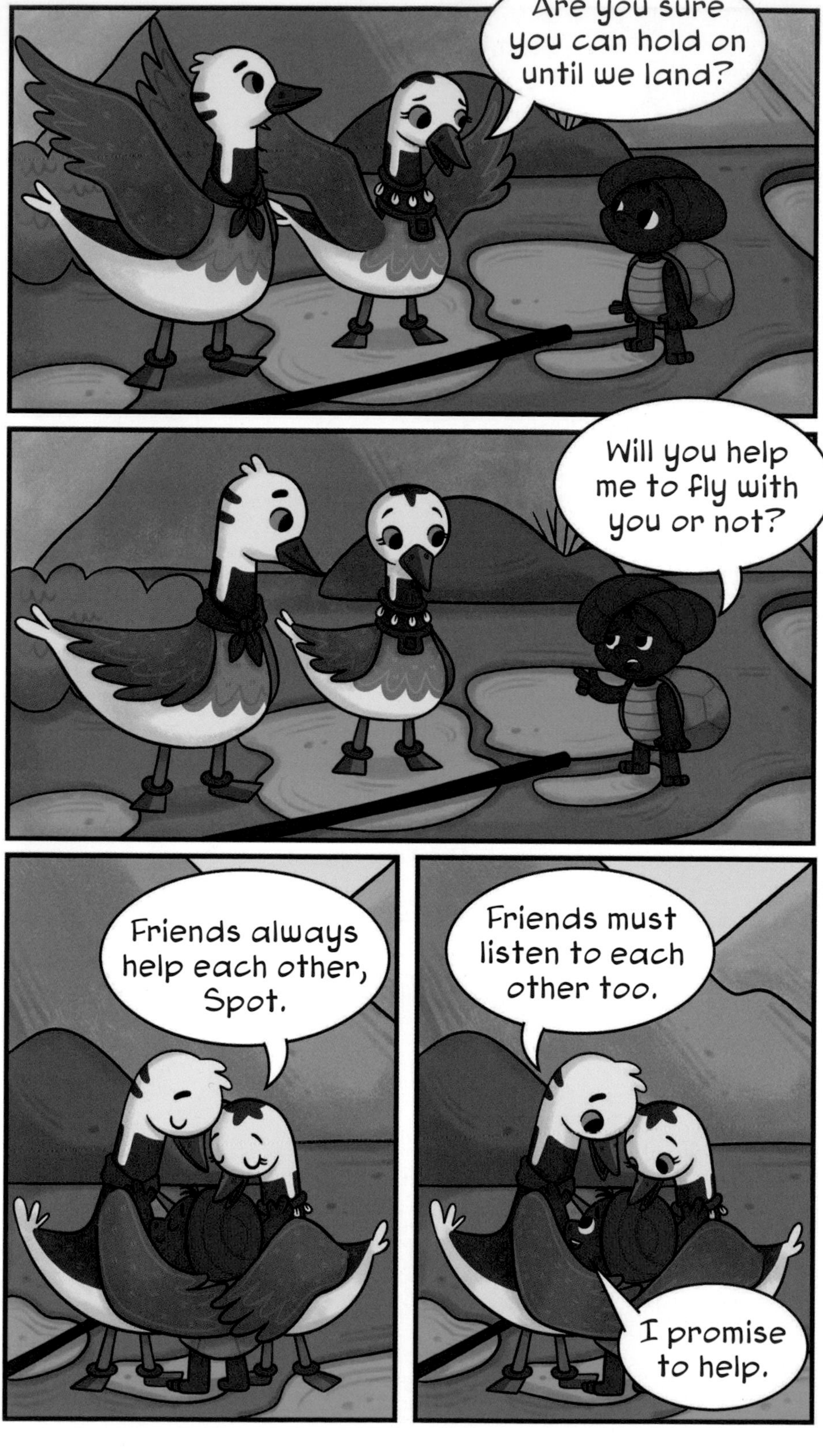
Are you sure you can hold on until we land?
Will you help me to fly with you or not?
Friends always help each other, Spot.
Friends must listen to each other too.
I promise to help.

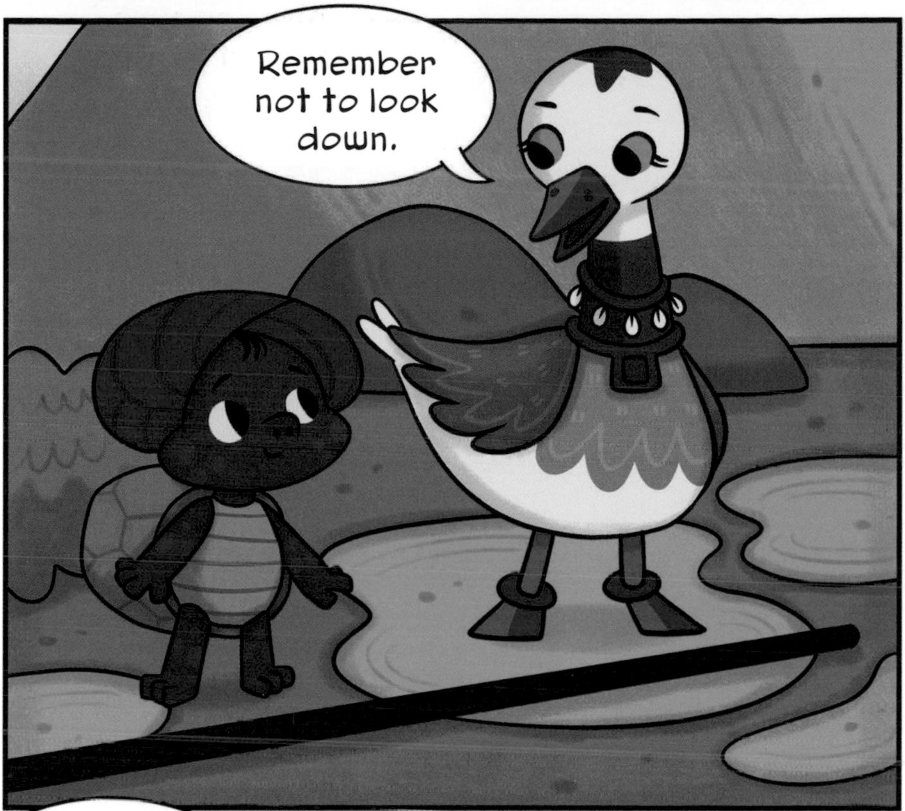
Remember
not to look
down.

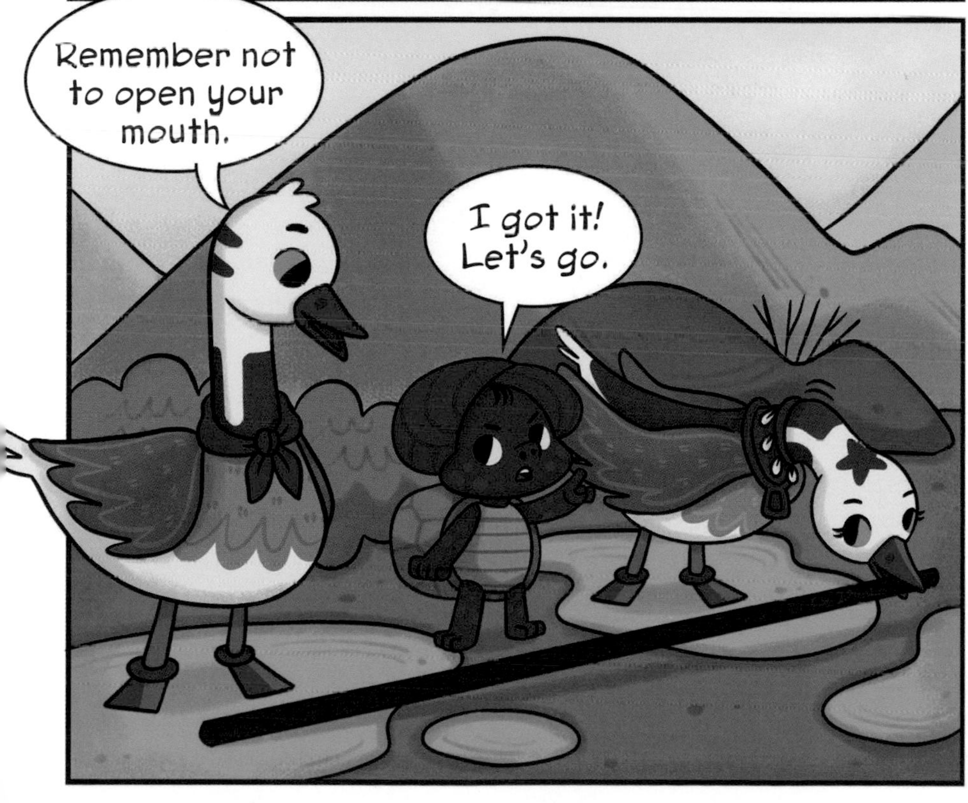
Remember not
to open your
mouth.
I got it!
Let's go.

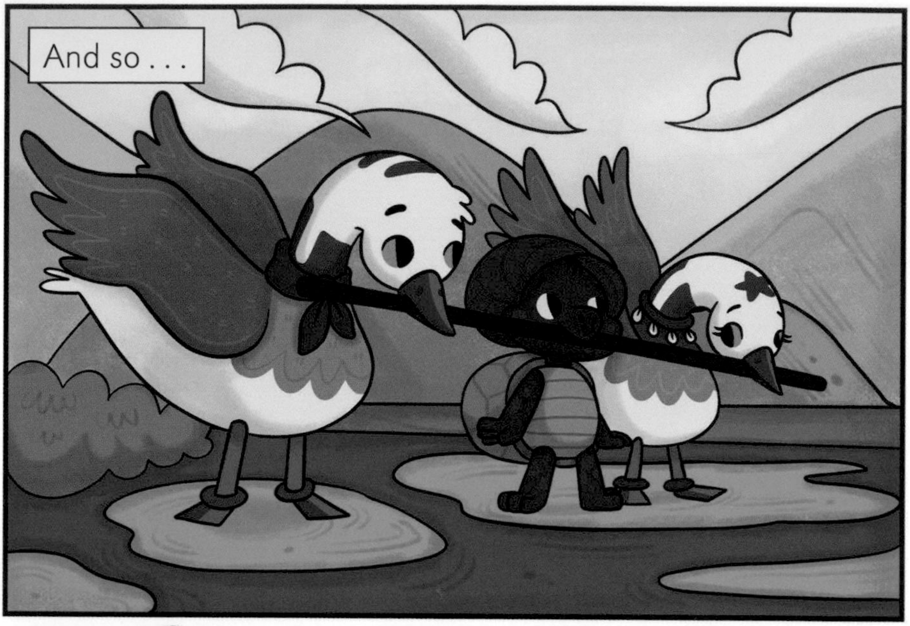
And so . . .

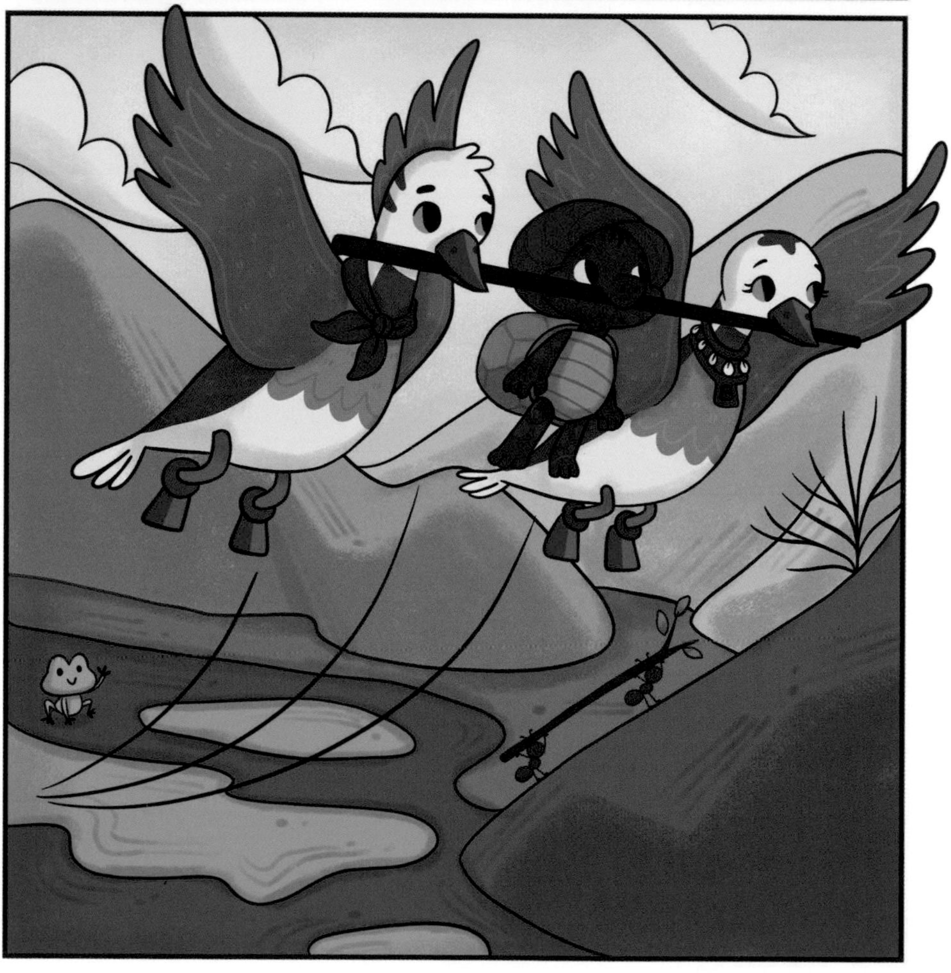

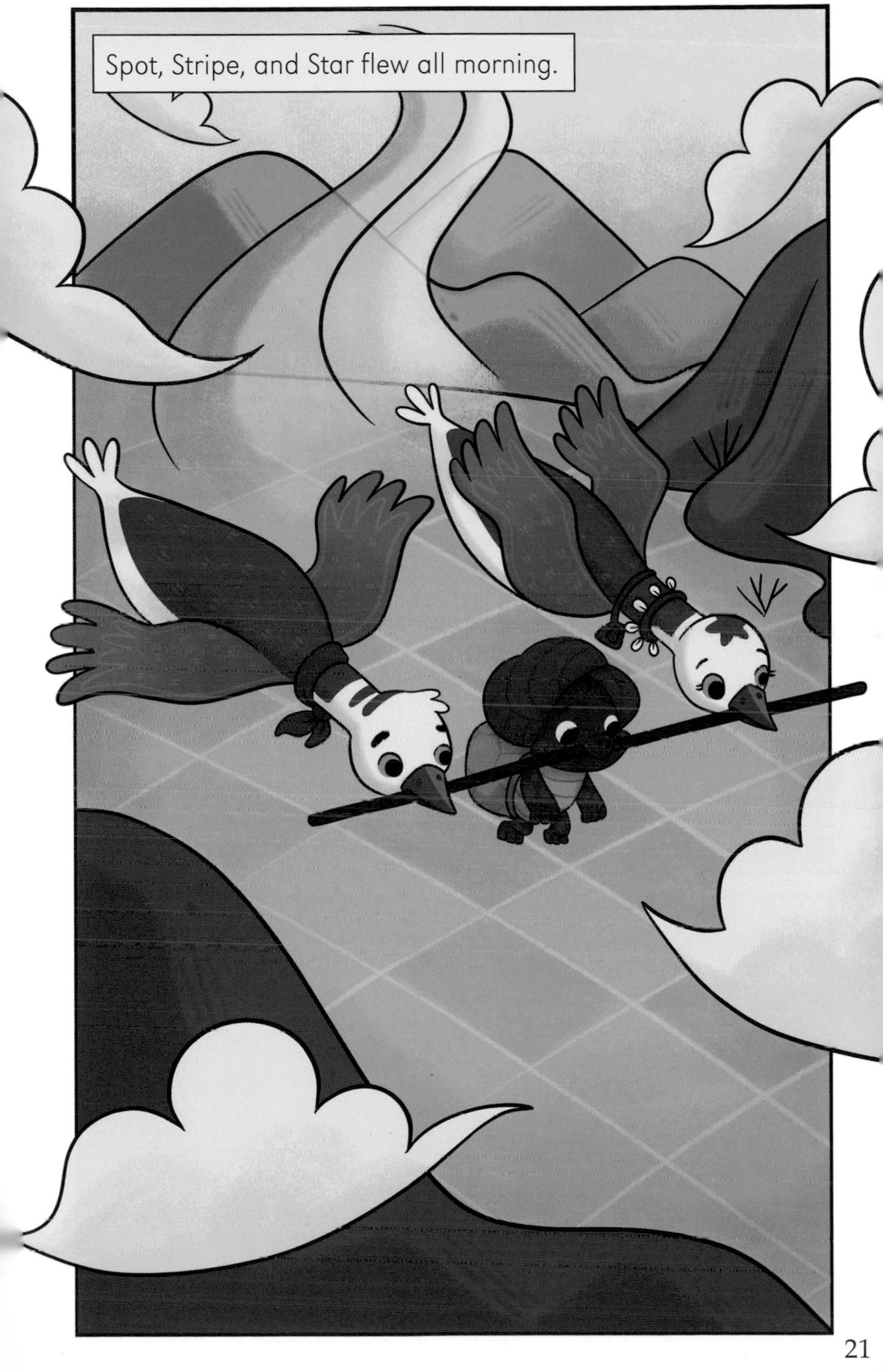
Spot, Stripe, and Star flew all morning.

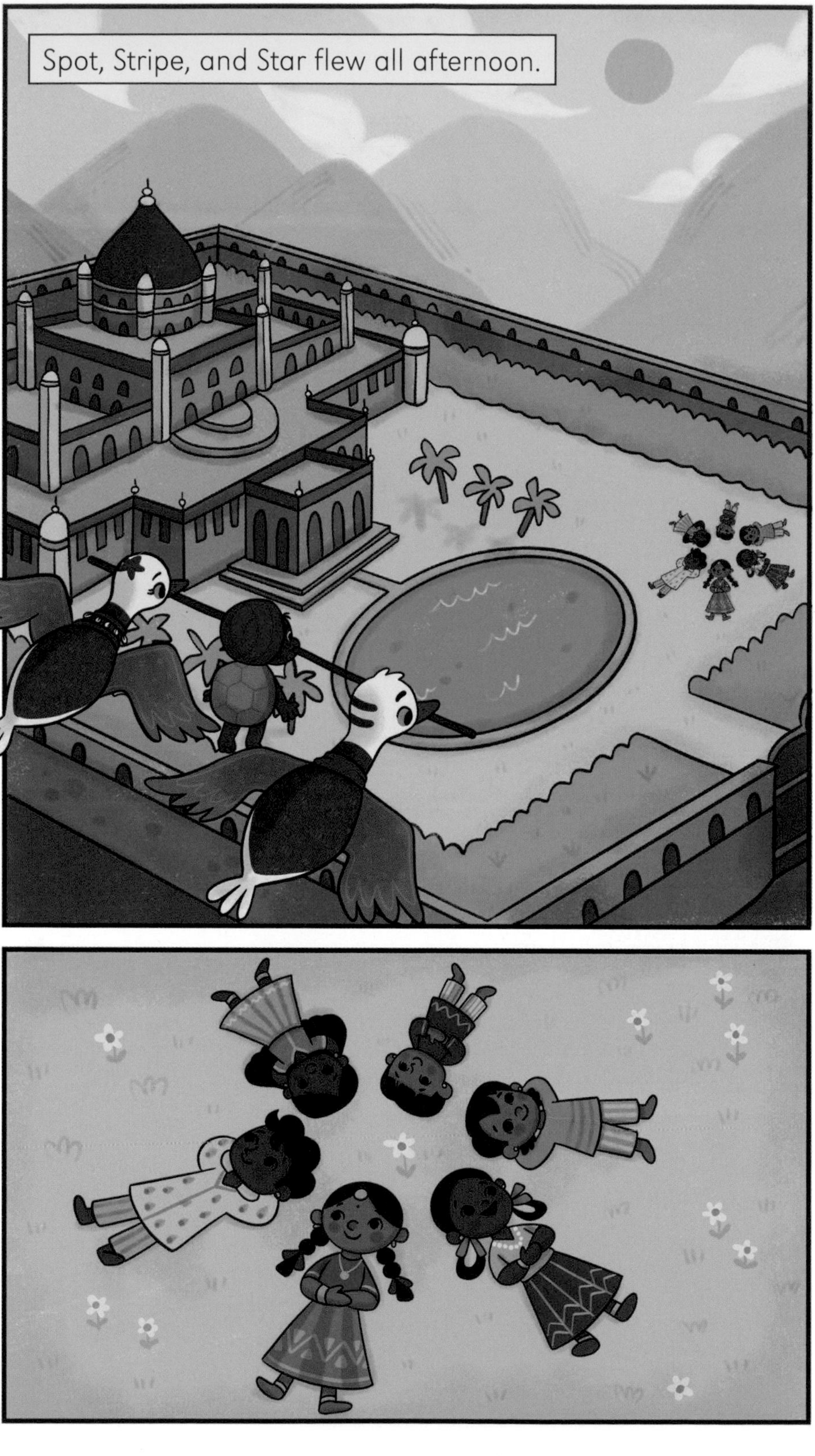
Spot, Stripe, and Star flew all afternoon.

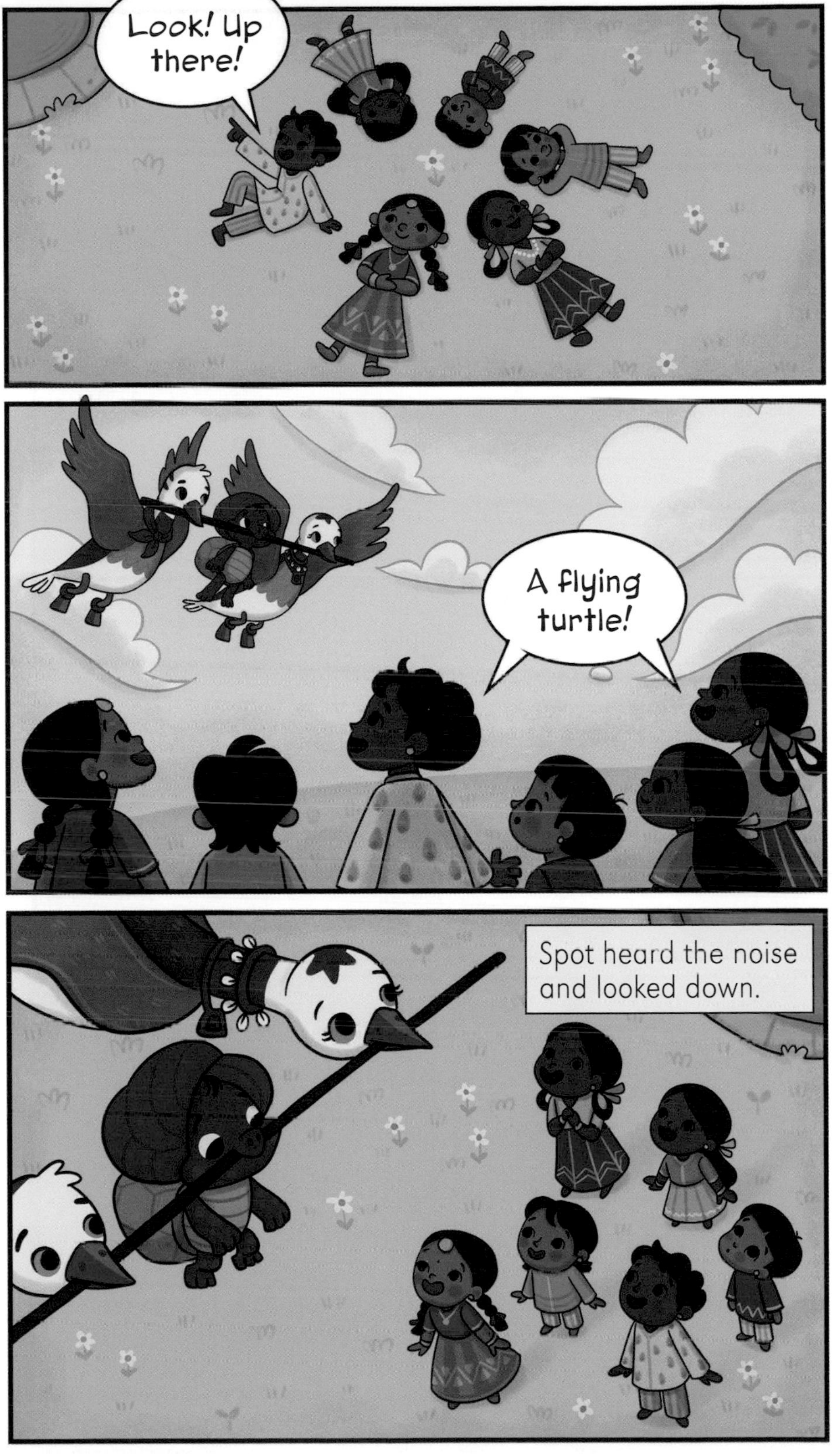
Look! Up there!
A flying turtle!
Spot heard the noise and looked down.

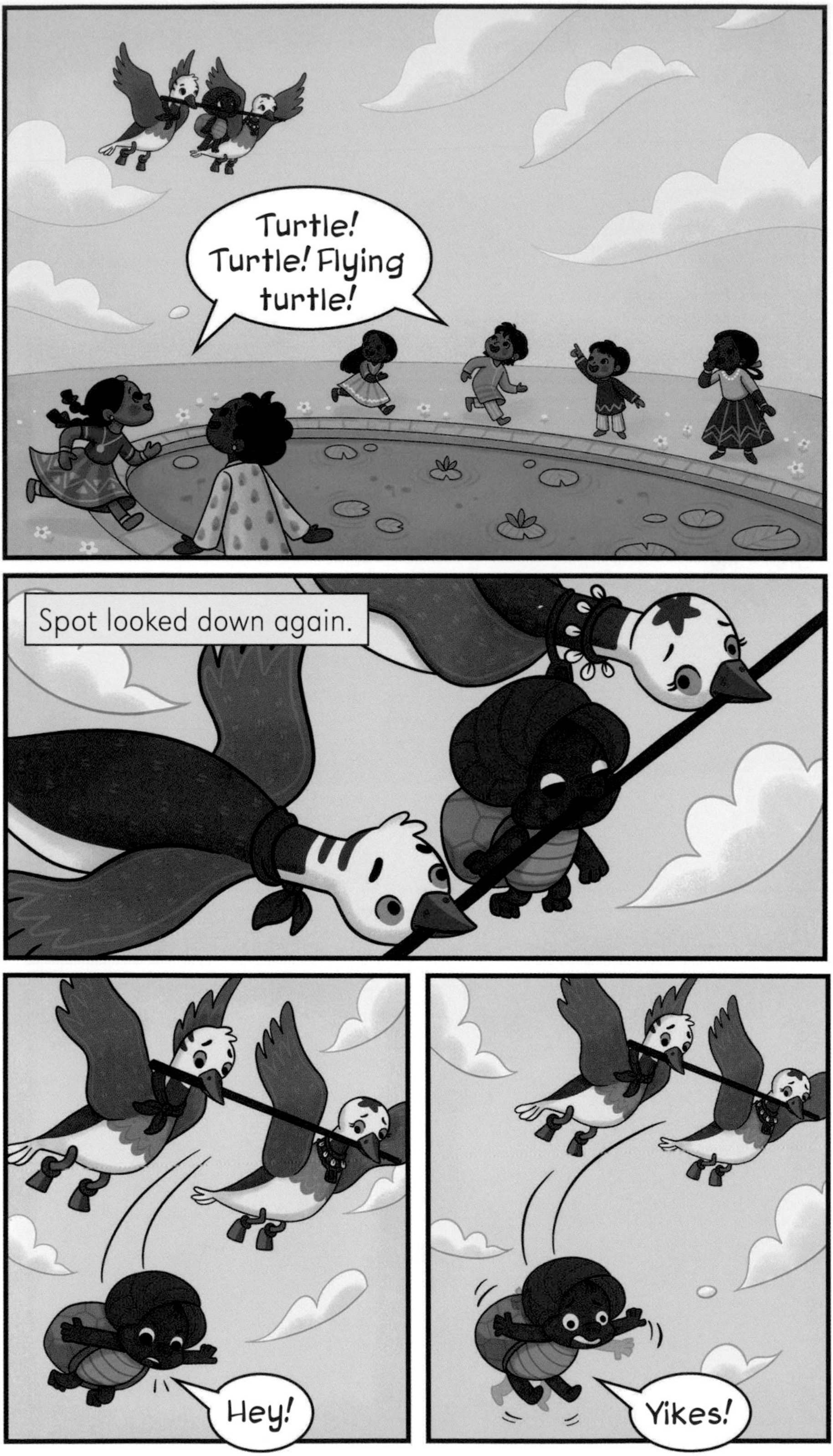
Turtle! Turtle! Flying turtle!
Spot looked down again.
Hey!
Yikes!

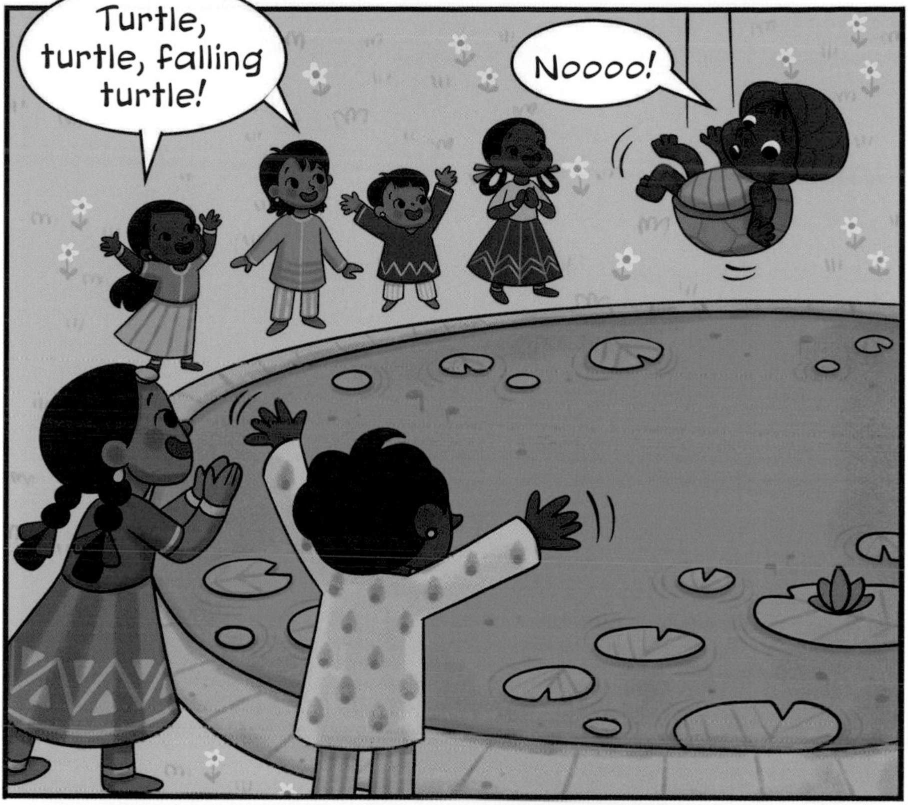
Turtle, turtle, falling turtle!
Noooo!

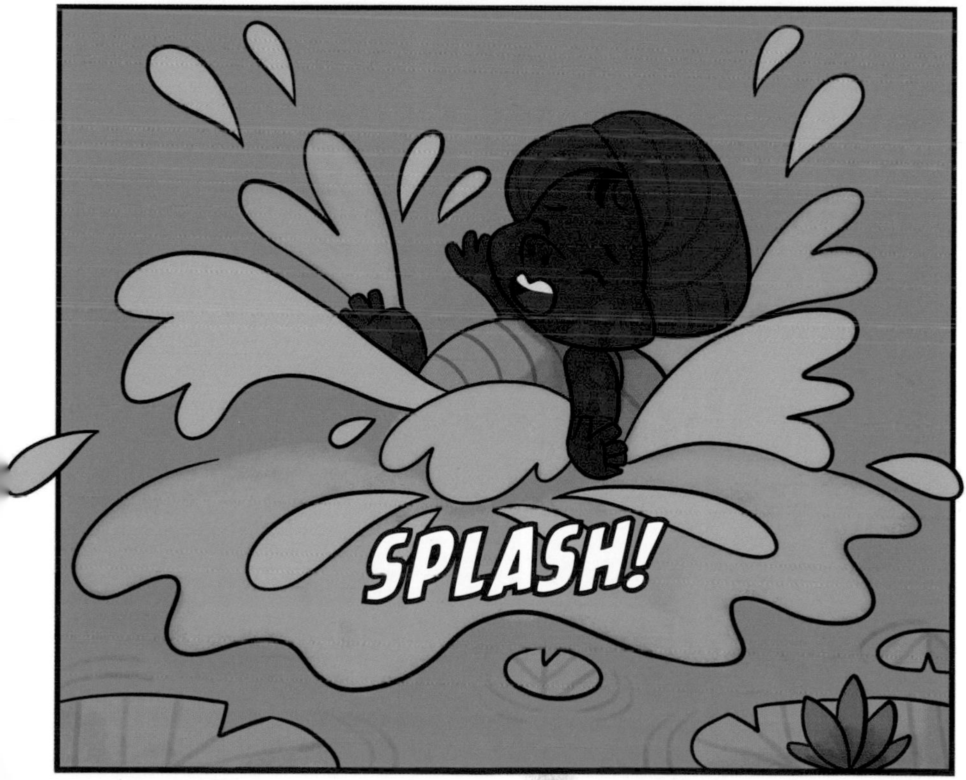
SPLASH!

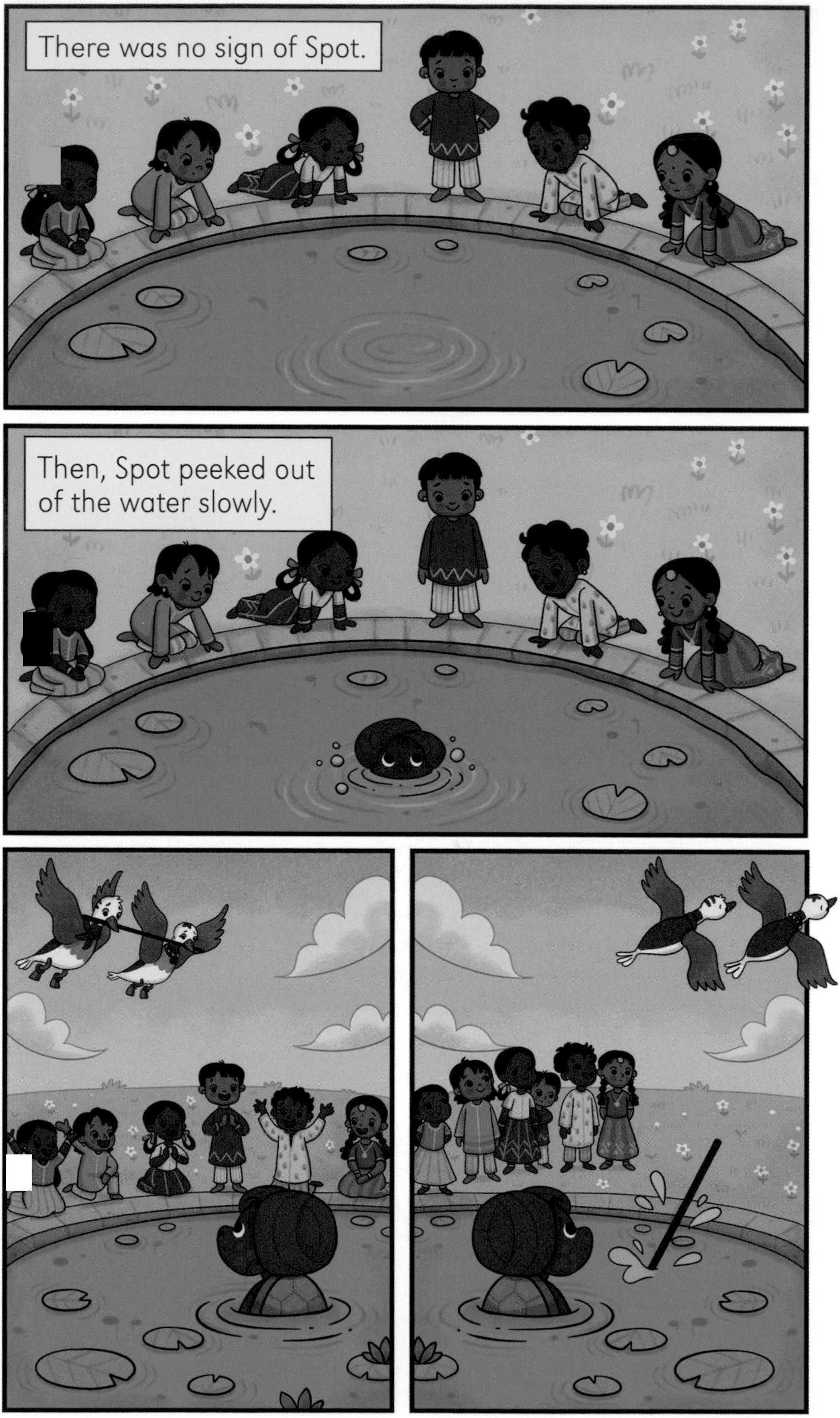
There was no sign of Spot.
Then, Spot peeked out of the water slowly.

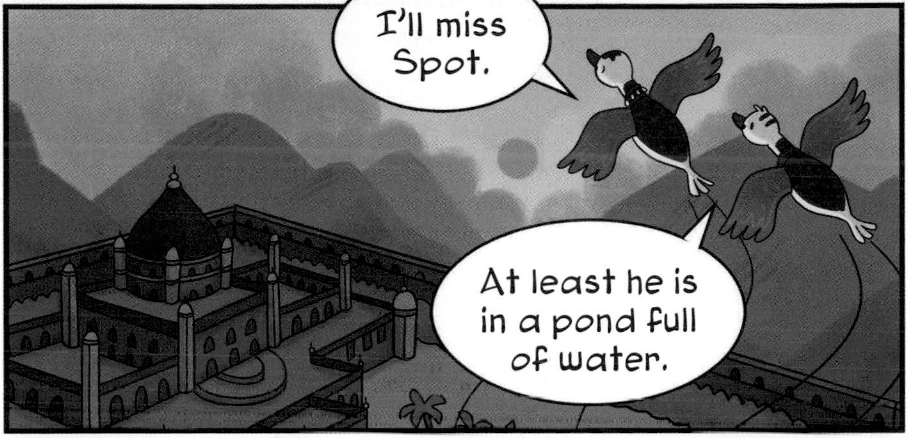
I'll miss Spot.
At least he is in a pond full of water.

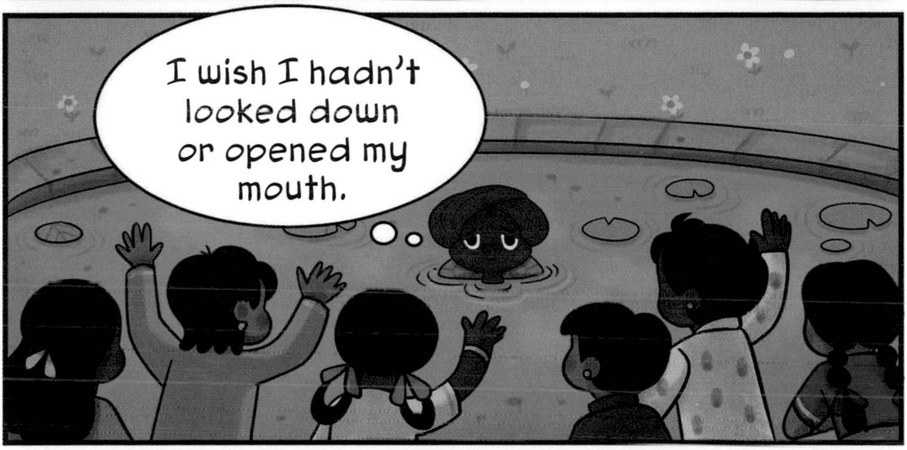
I wish I hadn't looked down or opened my mouth.

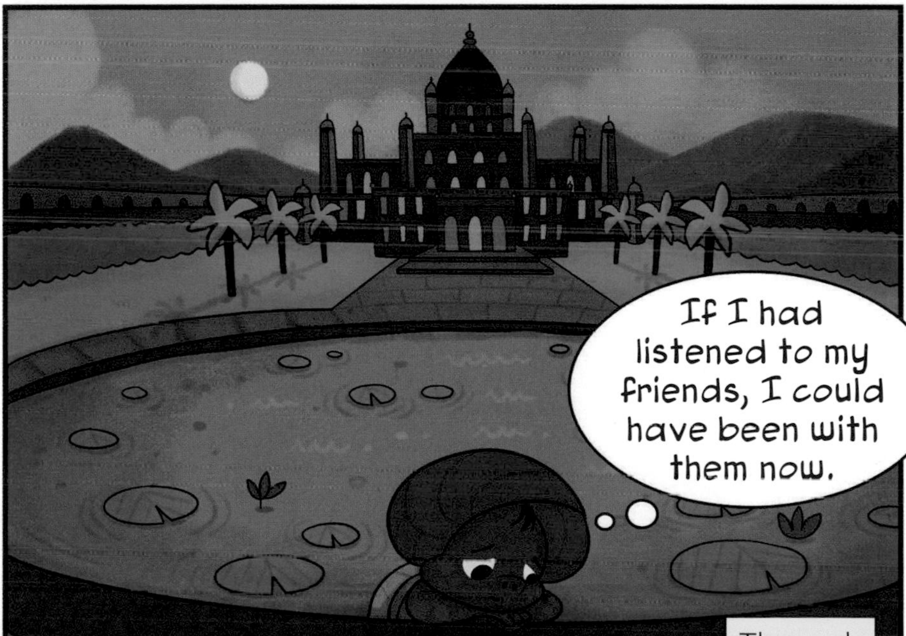
If I had listened to my friends, I could have been with them now.
The end.

WRITING PROMPTS

1. At the end of the tale, Spot wishes he had listened to the geese. Do you agree? Why or why not?

2. Discuss some other ways Spot could have traveled from one lake to the next. Let your imagination run wild!

3. Look back through the illustrations in this book. What is your favorite illustration and why?

DISCUSSION QUESTIONS

1. The original tale of the "Turtle and the Geese" began in India. Research more about India, and then write down a few of the most interesting facts about this country.

2. Folktales were often told aloud before they were ever written down. Think about a story your parents, teachers, or friends have told you in the past. Then try to write down that story from memory.

3. What happens next? Write a sequel, or second part, to this tale. Do Spot, Star, and Stripe stay friends? You decide!

GLOSSARY

beyond (bi-YOND)—on the far side of something

eureka (yur-REE-kuh)—used to express excitement when a discovery has been made

faraway (FAR-uh-WAY)—very distant or remote

gander (GAN-dur)—a male goose

kingdom (KING-duhm)—a country that has a king or queen as its ruler

palace (PAL-iss)—a large, grand residence for a king, queen, or other ruler

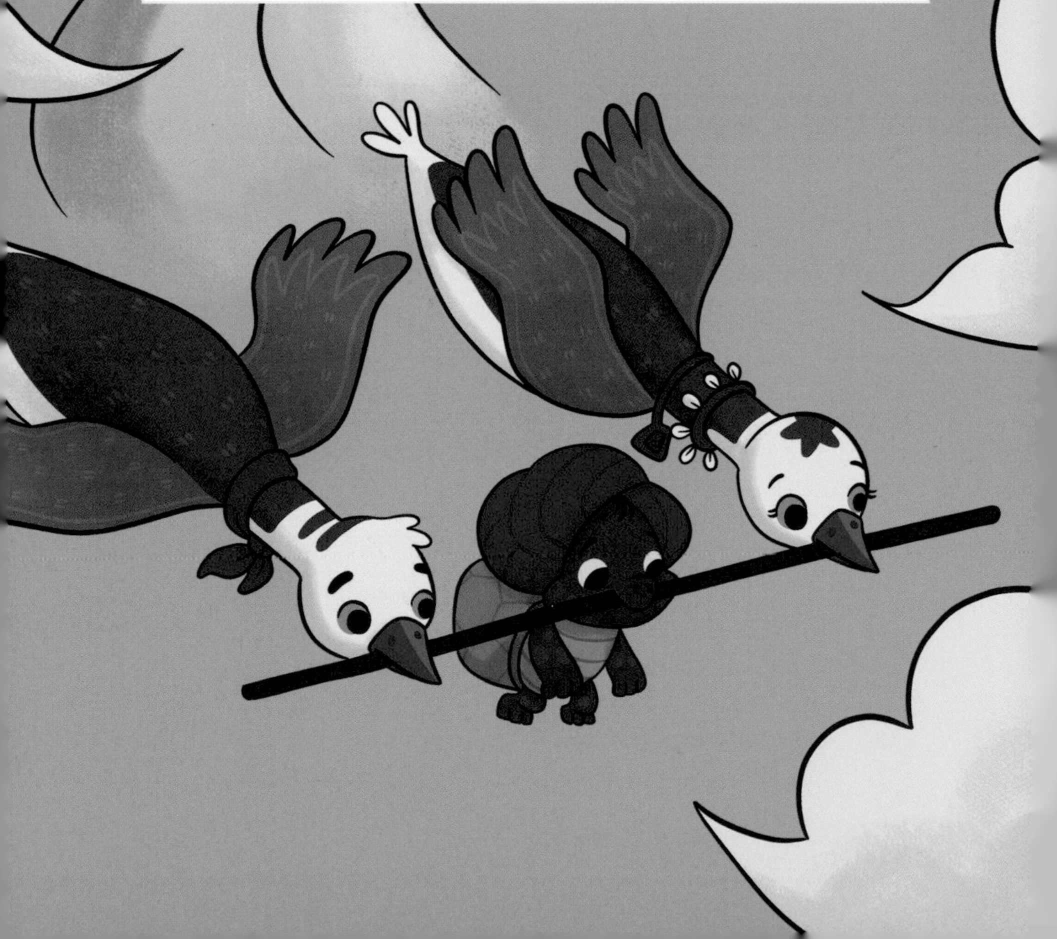

ABOUT THE AUTHOR

Chitra Soundar is an internationally published author of over 60 books for children. She is also an oral storyteller and writer of many things. Chitra writes picture books and fiction for young readers and for children's digital media including audio and TV. Her stories are inspired by folktales from India, Hindu mythology, and her travels around the world. Her books have been published in the UK, US, India, and Singapore and translated into Chinese, German, French, Japanese, and Thai.

ABOUT THE ILLUSTRATOR

Darshika lives with her family in Mumbai, India. She loves drawing characters in vibrant scenes and adorning them with emotions. Her art is majorly inspired by travels and childhood memories. She spends her free time bird-watching and reading books.

R[redacted]AD ALL THE AMAZING DISCOVER GRAPHICS BOOKS!

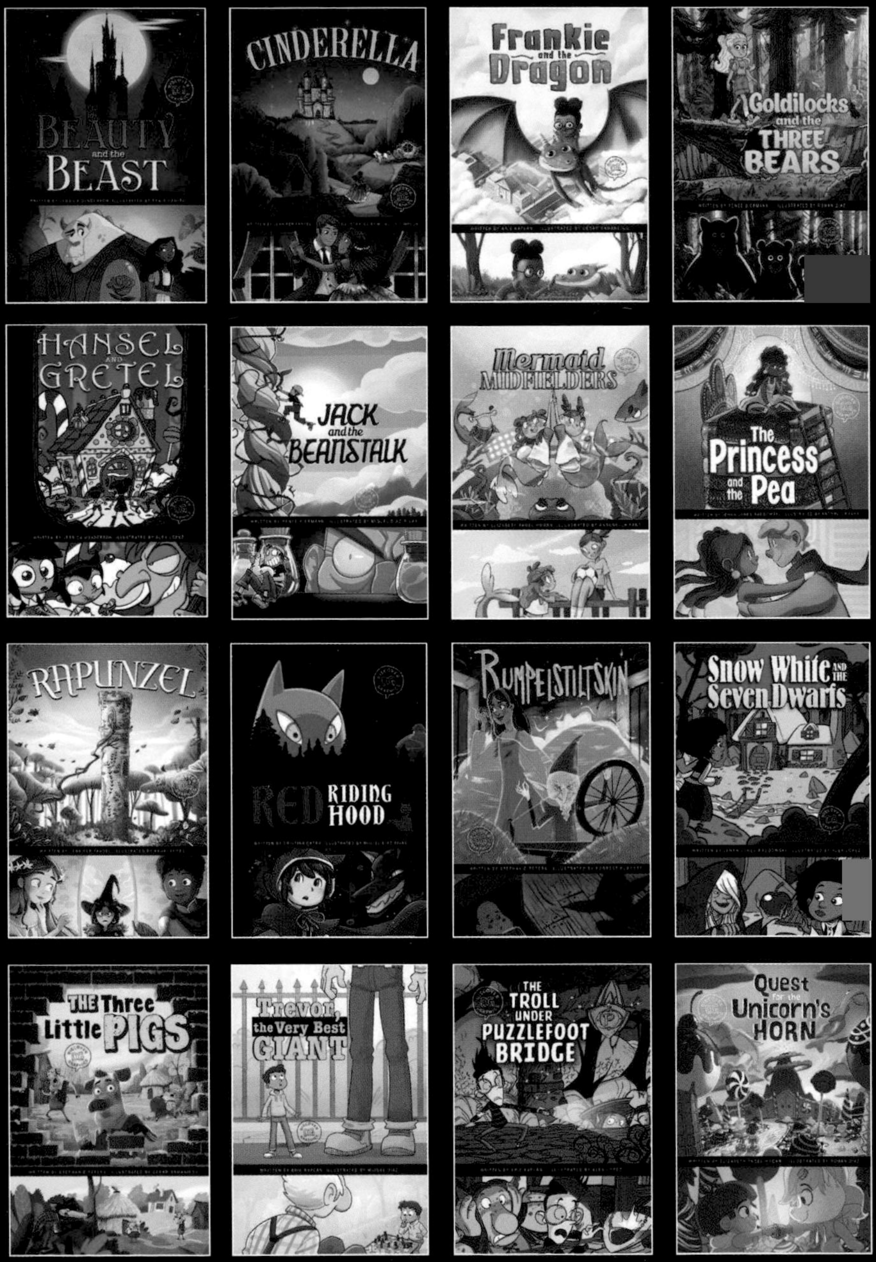
Beauty and the Beast
Cinderella
Frankie and the Dragon
Goldilocks and the Three Bears
Hansel and Gretel
Jack and the Beanstalk
Mermaid Midfielders
The Princess and the Pea
Rapunzel
Red Riding Hood
Rumpelstiltskin
Snow White and the Seven Dwarfs
The Three Little Pigs
Trevor, the Very Best Giant
The Troll Under Puzzlefoot Bridge
Quest for the Unicorn's Horn